# THE PORCH
## AND THE
# PROMISE

### A Journey of Faith on the Quiet Farm

The Porch and the Promise

ISBN: 9798284816264 (paperback)

First Edition

Printed in the United States of America imprint
independently published.

*Dedication:*

**To those who prayed for me when I
didn't have the strength to pray for
myself— thank you.
Your faith carried me farther than you know.
This is your harvest too.**

*"Those who sow with tears will reap with songs of joy.
Those who go out weeping, carrying seed to sow,
will return with songs of joy, carrying sheaves
with them."*
**—Psalm 126:5–6**

# THE PORCH AND THE PROMISE: *A JOURNEY OF FAITH ON THE QUIET FARM*

*Ashley Gill*

## *A Note from the Author*

Dear Reader,

Though The Porch and the Promise is a fictional story, it comes from a very real place in my heart — shaped by my life as a deaf woman living on a peaceful farm where prayer, worship, and discipleship are part of my everyday life rhythm.

I authored this story to share a glimpse of what it looks like when we open our homes, our hearts, and our lives to the presence of Jesus. I believe healing can happen around a kitchen table, deliverance can come under a quiet sky, and deep friendships can form in the most ordinary places — even a porch.

My prayer is that as you read, something stirs in you — hope, faith, longing, or even tears — and that you come away reminded of God's love, power, and purpose for your life.

There is room on the porch for you, too.

With love and
faith,
*Ashley Gill*

# 1. Golden Silence

(With Praise to the Heavenly Father)

The sun was just beginning to dip behind the hills when I stepped onto the porch, the sky glowing like it had been kissed by heaven. I wiped my hands on my worn white cotton shirt warm from work, a little sore, but deeply content. The smell of fresh hay and earth clung to my skin.

The chickens had already settled in, tucked safely in their coop. Their gentle clucks were familiar and comforting. I had signed **"goodnight"** to each one as always, and even though they didn't speak my language, they understood my love.

My dogs—four in all—rested around I like a living quilt: Milo, always curious; Sweetpea, the gentle one; Boots, the watchman; and Harriet, old and faithful. They wagged their tails as I passed, then stretched out again, calm because I was calm.

I sat down in my favorite rocking chair on the patio, the wood smooth under my palms. The cup of tea I brought with me warmed my fingers, but my heart was warmed by something deeper.

As I looked out over the fields glowing gold in the last light of day, a wave of thankfulness rose in me like a song.

I signed a quiet prayer with my hands.

**"Thank You, Lord."**

**"Thank You for the breath in my body."**
**"For this farm, for peace, for the dogs, the chickens, the sky."**
**"For another day to be in Your creation."**

I couldn't hear the wind, but I could feel it brush my cheeks like the whisper of angels. The sunset spread out in majesty across the horizon, and in that moment, I felt it— God's presence in everything. In the colors. In the stillness. In the breath of my dogs sleeping beside me. In my own heart, steady and full.

Tears came to my eyes, not from sadness, but from joy too deep for words.

I signed again, slowly, and reverent:
**"You are faithful, Lord. Always."**
**"Thank You for blessing me with this life."**

As the sun finally dipped below the hills, I sat in the holy silence. A moment just for me and my Heavenly Father. A shared secret between me and the sky.

And when I finally rose to go inside, the stars began to appear—one by one, like tiny nods from heaven.

Tomorrow will come with new chores, new joys, muddy paws, warm eggs, and morning praise.

But tonight, I had golden silence, God's peace, and a grateful heart.

## 2. Rooted in Grace

Morning mist still clung to the fields when I stepped outside, boots crunching softly on the gravel path. The dogs trotted alongside me, tails wagging, breath puffing little clouds into the cool air.

The garden waited—rich soil, rows of green reaching upward, kissed by dew.

I signed a quiet **"thank You"** to the sky before I stepped into it. This was my sacred place.

3

A place where prayers did not need to be spoken out loud, because my hands, my work, and my heart were always speaking to God.

I pulled on my gloves, and my day began. Peas and beans to harvest. Kale to rinse. Basil and lemon balm to snip and dry for my teas. I moved gently, knowing each plant like an old friend. My garden wasn't perfect—but it was *alive*, and it was *blessed*.

Years ago, I didn't know how to grow anything. I was uncertain in my faith then; too. I was unsure if I could hear God's voice without actual sound. But as seasons passed, and as seeds turned to life in my hands, something in my soul took root.

I realized: God's voice was *everywhere*. In the way the tomatoes leaned toward the sun. In the wind as it bent the mint. In the joy of the dogs racing through the open field. In my own heartbeat when, I paused in the garden and lifted my hands to the sky.

Now, every harvest was an answered prayer.

I knelt, hands in the soil, and felt the pulse of the earth— steady and giving. I signed in praise; eyes closed for a moment.

**"Thank You for teaching me through the garden, Lord."**

**"For growing me the way You grow everything—
gently, daily, with love."**

After filling your baskets, I sat on the patio with my tea—
fresh peppermint and lavender today. The sun was just
beginning to climb high. The dogs rested at my feet. I
pulled out my small Bible, well-worn and full of notes.

I traced the verse; I had underlined just days before:
**"I am the vine; you are the branches..."** *(John
15:5)* And I smiled because, I understood that now—
deeply.
Everything I needed, I found when I stayed rooted in Him.

The world was noisy, but my life was quiet and full. And in
that quiet, God had met me, repeatedly. I wasn't just
growing vegetables anymore. I was growing **stronger in
faith**, richer in spirit, and full of holy joy.

## 3. Storm Season

The sky turned gray before I finished my morning garden rounds. I felt it in the wind— different than usual, urgent, electric. The chickens were restless. The dogs barked more than they usually did.

I looked toward the sky and signed, **"Peace, Lord."** But my spirit stirred.

By late afternoon, the storm hit. Heavy rain lashed the fields. Wind tore through the trees. I moved fast, guiding the chickens into the secured part of the coop, gathering the dogs inside. Thunder shook the house. I couldn't hear it—but I could *feel* it, deep in my chest like a second heartbeat.

And then, the lights flickered. Went out. Everything fell into darkness.

I sat in the candlelight, my Bible book on my lap, dogs curled around me. I felt the silence so deeply now—not the silence of being deaf, but the silence of the unknown. Would the garden survive? Would my crops hold? I had planted so much—hope, food for others, teas for my body and soul. I had poured myself into the soil.

I could feel the fear rising, creeping up like weeds.

My hands shook as I signed the words:
**"I trust You, Lord."**
**"Even now. Even if I lose the harvest. You are my Provider."**

I began to weep—not from panic, but surrender. It wasn't the kind of storm I could stop. But I knew who held the sky.

The next morning, the storm passed. Trees were bent, some branches broken, puddles deep in the fields—but the garden stood.

Bent. Bruised. But alive.

I stepped out into the light, hands trembling, heart still raw. I walked through the rows. Some vegetables were washed out. A few herbs were torn. But most of it—somehow—had held on.

I dropped to my knees, hands in the earth, tears falling silently down my cheeks.

**"Thank You, Jesus."**
**"Not just for what was saved—but for showing me You are with me in the storm." "I am still rooted in You."**

That evening, I made tea from what was left of the chamomile and rosemary. I sat on the patio, wrapped in a quilt, a candle beside me. The dogs lay quietly at my feet. The chickens, shaken but unharmed, clucked drowsily in the coop.

I looked at the sky, streaked in soft pink and gold, and lifted my hands again in silent praise.

I had weathered a storm in the field and in my faith.

And in both, I found the same truth:

**God never left you.**

**Not for one single moment.**

**And He never will.**

## 4. Fellowship on the Farm

It was a day I had prayed over for weeks—clear skies, warm sun, and friends arriving down the gravel road in cars full of laughter. I stood on the porch, an apron dusted with flour, dogs wagging wildly at my side.

My garden had been prepared with love: herbs bundled in jars, tomatoes lined in neat baskets, fresh bread resting under a clean cloth. The chickens seemed to sense the excitement, clucking with extra cheer. Today was not just a visit. It was *a fellowship*. A gathering of sisters in Christ, souls who had prayed with me, lifted me, and walked beside me through life's quiet and stormy seasons.

One by one, they stepped out with arms wide and smiles even wider— Women of all kinds, each with her own testimony, her own faith journey. Some signed like me, others spoke, but all shared one language today: **praise**.

After the hugs, after the dogs settled (mostly), I gathered outside near the garden, around a long table draped with a simple cloth, and flowers cut fresh that morning, and plates already filling with food.

One sister brought sweet potato pie, another fried fish and greens, and another iced hibiscus tea that glowed ruby in the sun.

We all bowed our heads, some speaking aloud, others singing quietly, all offering thanks.

**"Thank You, Lord, for this day."**
**"For this food, these hands, this sisterhood."**
**"Thank You for joy that runs deeper than words."**

And then came the laughter. The stories. The music. One sister brought a guitar, and another lifted her hands in worship. I joined in, signing the lyrics as they sang:

*"Way maker, miracle worker, promise keeper..."*

The sun was warm on my skin as tears rose in my eyes—not from sadness, but from the overwhelming goodness of God. I stood in the middle of my garden, among herbs and tomatoes, surrounded by sisters, and signed the words:

**"This is holy ground."**

Later, as the sun dipped low and the sky turned golden, my favorite time—we all sat quietly, arms touching, shoulders leaning together.

And in the hush of sunset,

someone whispered: **"There's so**

**much peace here. I feel God**

**in this place."** I smiled, eyes

still on the sky, and signed:

**"He lives here. In the garden. In the silence. In us."**

As fireflies blinked to life and my dogs curled at the feet of my friends, a soft hymn rose again:

*"Great is Thy faithfulness..."*

And as you signed the chorus into the air, you knew—this was not just my farm.

It was my ministry.

## 5. A Place to Begin Again

It started with a simple question.

**"Can I come visit?"**

She was a new believer—quiet, withdrawn, someone I'd met only once during a house fellowship, livestream gathering. She had found me online through a mutual friend and said something about my farm, my peace, how she couldn't stop thinking about it.

**"I'm trying to believe,"** she had written.

**"But I don't know how to let go of everything I've been holding. I'm tired. Angry. I need to forgive—but I don't know how."**

I didn't hesitate. **"Yes. Come."**

When she arrived, her eyes were heavy with old pain. She barely spoke. I embraced her gently, hands signing welcome, and pointed her to a quiet guest room in my house. The dogs greeted her like an old friend. The chickens clucked from a distance. The wind was soft that day—almost like the land itself was whispering *"You're safe here."*

I didn't rush her. I gave her space. But I invited her into my rhythm.

Each morning, she joined me in the garden—hands in the dirt, silence between me. At first, she looked unsure, her movements stiff, her spirit closed like a fist. But over the days, something began to shift.

She watched me pray before harvesting mint. She saw how I signed blessings over the tea I made. I gave her a small journal and signed, **"Write anything. Questions. Prayers. Even anger. God can handle it."**

One evening, as the sun sank into its golden hush, she finally spoke.

**"How did you forgive?"**
Her voice cracked as she asked it.

I took her hands, steady and slow, and signed with grace:

**"It wasn't all at once. It took time. Tears. Truth. I gave my pain to the Lord, piece by piece."**

**"I couldn't do it without Him. And I couldn't heal while still carrying the weight of others' wrongs. I had to choose freedom."**

She cried then, quietly, and hard. And I let her. No fixing, no preaching. Just presence.

That night, we prayed together under the stars. I signed my praise, and she whispered to herself. The dogs lay around my feet like a circle of peace. The Spirit of God wrapped around me like a shawl.

The next morning, she asked to pray before picking herbs.

By the end of the week, her eyes were clearer. She laughed for the first time—laughing when a chicken hopped into her lap and refused to move. She danced in the garden, arms raised, free. And on her last night, she whispered, **"I still have work to do. But I believe now. I believe He wants to heal me."**

I smiled, tears in my eyes, and signed:

**"He already started."**

As she left, she turned and said, **"I want to come back. I want to learn more. Grow deeper. Maybe help others like me."**

And I knew in my spirit:

The farm wasn't just a quiet retreat. It was a place where roots went deep—into soil and into souls. A place where new believers could begin again, where healing wasn't rushed, and where forgiveness grew like wildflowers.

**Because God had made it holy.**

**And I had made it home.**

## 6. Breaking Chains with Maggie

It had been three months since Maggie first came to my farm.

Now she was back—different. Her smile came easier, and her steps were steadier. But in her eyes, I still saw it: the weight. The battle wasn't over yet. Healing had begun, but deeper wounds were surfacing. Old strongholds, lies she'd carried since childhood. Shame she hadn't known how to name.

When she hugged me on the porch, she held on longer than before. **"I'm ready,"** she whispered.
 **"I want to be free—for real."**

I had already been praying. And I'd already invited the right women.

By evening, my kitchen was full of warm, holy laughter—pots of soup simmering, cornbread baking, mugs steeping with herbs from the garden. But more than that, it was full of *faith*.

Three of my closest sisters in Christ were women of prayer, women who had fought their own wars in silence and come out stronger. Each one had brought her Bible, her testimony, and her full heart.

When the sun went down, I moved to the patio, where lanterns flickered and the air was still. Maggie sat in the center, nervous, clutching her journal.

I began with worship—soft, gentle songs lifted to the Lord. One of the sisters sang while another signed the words with flowing grace. Maggie closed her eyes and listened, her heart opening like a flower at dawn.

Then came the prayer.

I gathered around her, and my hands gently laid. No performance. Just holy authority.

One sister began to speak Scripture:

**"The Spirit of the Lord is upon me... to proclaim liberty to the captives..."** *(Luke 4:18)*

Another began to pray in the Spirit, words like rushing water.

I knelt beside Maggie and signed, slow and strong:

**"The chains are not stronger than Jesus. You are not who the enemy says you are. You are loved. You are chosen. You are free."**

At first, Maggie trembled. She began to cry, then sob, then weep so deeply it shook her whole body. Shame poured out like poison. Memories surfaced. Pain that had never been spoken.

And then—it broke.

She gasped, like a deep breath returning after years underwater. Her shoulders dropped. Her face softened. And she opened her eyes, glowing with peace.

She looked around at all of us, trembling but smiling.  **"It's gone. It's really gone."**

We all began to cry and laugh and praise—tears turned into hallelujahs.

**"Thank You, Jesus."**
**"Thank You for freedom."**
**"Thank You for Maggie's new beginning."**

That night, I lit a fire outside. I let her burn pages from her journal—pages full of lies she had believed about herself. She watched them turn to ash and then lifted her face to the stars.

I wrapped her in a quilt and handed her a fresh cup of peppermint tea.

As I sat in the glow, someone began singing again:

 *"I am no longer a slave to fear... I am a child of God."*

And Maggie joined in—her voice clear, her eyes bright, her soul free.

I looked around at my sisters, my farm, my garden in the moonlight, and gave thanks to my Heavenly Father.

**This was what your land was for.**
 **Not just peace.**
 **Not just beauty.**
 **But *deliverance*.**
 **The breaking of chains.**
 **And the rising of daughters.**

## 7. A Disciple in Bloom

Maggie started visiting the farm every weekend, just like she said she would. At first, she came quietly, still tender from healing, still learning how to walk in this new freedom. But each time she stepped onto my land, something in her seemed to brighten.

I could see it in her eyes. In her smile. In the way she lingered near the herb beds, gently touching each plant as if it was part of her story.

She followed me through the rhythms of the farm:
 Feeding chickens.

 Pulling weeds.
 Picking thyme and mint for tea.
 Reading Scripture aloud on the porch while the dogs dozed at our feet.

But most of all, she followed me as I followed **Jesus**.

I never forced it. I just lived the Gospel—openly, joyfully. She watched how I prayed before planting. How I signed blessings over the harvest. How I worshiped quietly as I folded laundry or stirred soup.

And slowly, Maggie began to mirror it. Not in imitation, but in transformation.

She brought her Bible each time now underlined and marked with scribbled prayers. She memorized verses and asked deeper questions:
 **"How do I hear His voice?"**
 **"How do I love like Him when people hurt me again?"**
 **"How do I know I'm called?"**

I told her the truth:
 **"You already are.**
 **You're called to love Him.**
 **To follow Him.**
 **To become like Him.**
 **That's all the discipleship is. Step by step."**

On one golden afternoon, she joined me on the patio again, barefoot, and joyful. She held her mug of chamomile tea and said,

**"I think I'm changing. I feel... lighter. More like myself. Or maybe who I was always meant to be."** I smiled with tears in my eyes and signed:

**"You are becoming more like Jesus. That's what you're feeling. His Spirit alive in you."**

She looked out over the field, quiet for a while, then said:
**"I used to think I was too broken. Too complicated to be used by God. But now I know... this life—this peace—it's all grace. Every breath. Every moment."**

And I whispered inside my heart, **"Thank You, Heavenly Father.**

**For her.**

**For this place.**

**For the privilege of watching, You work."**

That night, as the sun melted into the hills and the chickens settled for sleep, I sat beside Maggie and opened my Bible to Psalm 103. She read it aloud, slowly, and tears slipped down her face again—not from pain this time, but from joy.

**"Bless the Lord, O my soul...  and**

**forget not all His benefits.**

**Who forgives all your iniquities, who heals**

**all your diseases... who redeems your life**

**from destruction..."**

When she finished, she looked at me and said,

**"This place... this farm... it's a garden for the soul.**

**And I don't just want to visit anymore.**

**I want to live like this—fully for Him.**

**Always."**

And at that moment, I saw it:


The fruit of faith.
The power of simple obedience.
The greatness of my Heavenly Father—right here, in the life of one healed, growing woman named Maggie.

Everything I had—my land, my time, my quiet life—belonged to **Him**.

And He had used it to bring a daughter home.

## 8. Maggie's Calling

Maggie had become part of my weekends like sunrise and tea. She no longer came just to receive it. Now she came ready to **serve**.

One Saturday morning, she showed up with two women in tow. **"This is Keisha, and this is Alondra,"** she signed with a warm smile. **"They're new in their faith. I told them about the farm... about you."**

I welcomed them with open arms. It reminded me of when Maggie first arrived — shy eyes, quiet hearts, unsure if there was a place for them in this kingdom of peace.

Now Maggie was the one offering peace.

She guided them through the herb garden, explaining how each plant helped with healing — chamomile for anxiety, lemon balm for rest, peppermint for clarity. She spoke gently, but with confidence. I watched her from the patio; my heart was swelling. She moved with Spirit now.

Later, the four of us sat beneath the old oak tree with our Bibles open, tea in hand. The dogs laid nearby, the breeze carried the scent of rosemary, and the chickens scratched softly in the distance.

Maggie shared her testimony.

**"I used to believe I was too broken.**

**But God met me here — in this quiet place.**

**He didn't just heal me.**

**He gave me purpose."**

Keisha cried. Alondra asked if she could come back next week.

And I knew: the farm had become something more.

**A sanctuary.**
**A discipleship center.**
**A womb for spiritual rebirth.**

That night, after the women had gone home, Maggie and I sat on the porch again under a sky bursting with stars. She turned to me and said:

**"I want to do more. Not just weekends. I want to help you full time. I think... maybe God wants me to stay."**

I smiled — not surprised. I had seen it coming. The Lord had already been stirring my heart.

**"This is His land,"** I signed.
**"And He's raising laborers in His harvest. You are one of them."**

Maggie nodded, eyes full of peace and purpose. **"Let's start something together. A place where women come not just to visit, but to learn, to heal, to grow deep roots in Christ."**

I looked at her, this once-wounded girl turned mighty woman of God, and whispered in your spirit:

**"He who began a good work in you will carry it on to completion..."** *(Philippians 1:6)*

And once again, I thanked my Heavenly Father.

For the healing.

For the calling.

 For every life that would be changed beneath the wide sky, in the quiet soil, and under the blessing of His name.

## 9. The Invitation: From the farm to the Nations

That evening, after a day of tending the garden and welcoming guests, I led Maggie into the newly finished guest bedroom.

The room was simple, peaceful — soft linens, handmade quilts, a Bible resting on the small table by the bed, and a window that opened toward the sunset. The scent of lavender from the sachet under the pillow filled the room.

**"This is your space now,"** I signed with a smile.

**"You're not just visiting anymore. You're part of this."**

Maggie's eyes welled with tears. She looked around the room, touched the quilt, then hugged me tightly.
 **"Thank you... I never thought I'd belong anywhere. But now I do."**

After she settled in, I made tea and sat with her on the porch beneath the stars. That's when I told her.

**"I'm going to North Carolina next month,"** I signed. **"It's a big gathering — a kickstart event. Believers from everywhere come together: men, women, new believers, and those who are still searching.**

**We worship, we pray, we teach, we serve, and many are delivered, healed, and filled with the Holy Spirit."**

Maggie's face lit up with wonder and nervous excitement.

**"You're inviting me?"**

I nodded.
 **"I believe the Lord wants you to see more. You've grown so much here, and now it's time to see what the wider Body of Christ looks like. What real discipleship looks like outside of the quiet."**

Over the next few weeks, Maggie helped prepare the farm for our short trip. But in the evenings, I shared stories of my past visits—of people set free, baptized in water and Spirit, of songs rising from hearts that once didn't know the name of Jesus.

And when the day came, I packed my Bibles, comfortable clothes, and anointing oil. I prayed over the land before I left, leaving it in the Father's hands.

## 10. The Fire in Carolina

The moment we arrived at the gathering; Maggie's eyes grew wide. There were hundreds of people — some singing, some weeping, some kneeling. The Spirit of God was moving everywhere, like wind across a field.

I stayed close to her side at first, guiding her gently.

The worship began — loud, bold, full of power. Maggie lifted her hands, tears running down her face. She didn't know the words to every song, but her heart understood every note.

Later, I joined a group of women and men praying over a young man who had never been in church before. He trembled, wept, and then shouted for joy as the Lord delivered him from torment.

Maggie watched, stunned, tears in her eyes.
 **"This is real,"** she whispered.
 **"It's not just stories. Jesus is really setting people free right now."**

By the second day, Maggie was laying hands on people herself, praying, weeping, praising.
Her prayers were simple but powerful:

 **"Jesus, show them You love them like You did for me."**

She hugged strangers like family. She sat with new believers and listened to their pain, offering the same peace she had once received.

One evening, I found her alone, looking out over a hill where people were being baptized in a nearby creek. She turned to me and said:

**"I didn't know the kingdom of God looked like this— so full, so alive. I thought it was just about quiet devotion. But it's also a movement. Power. Love that reaches everyone."**

I nodded, tears in my eyes.
 **"This is what it means to be a disciple. To walk where He sends. To carry peace, healing, and truth into the world. You're doing it now."**

That night, she danced in worship — barefoot, unashamed, laughing in the Spirit's joy, and I knew. The girl who once came broken and afraid now walked boldly in her calling.

**Not just a guest. Not just a helper.**
**But a daughter of the King.**
**A disciple of Jesus.**
**And a light to many.**

## 11. Return & Renewal

The North Carolina trip stirred something deep in Maggie. But when we both came back to the farm, it was time to **root** that fire in truth.

I knew revival wasn't just about outward signs — it was about a life *renewed*, moment by moment, under the lordship of Christ.

Over the next days, I sat with her each morning after feeding the animals. Bible open, tea warm in hand.

I taught her:

**"Your identity is not in what you *do* for the Lord.**

**It's in who you *are* in Him.**
**Chosen. Washed. Adopted. Loved."**

She listened closely. Took notes. Asked honest questions.
I also warned her gently:
**"Be watchful, daughter. When you start walking in**
**your purpose, the enemy may tempt you with pride.**
**But we stay low. We stayed surrendered. We stay close**
**to Jesus."**

Maggie nodded with new maturity in her eyes.

The following weekend, Maggie invited her old friends— Keisha
and Alondra—back to the farm. This time, she was the one
preparing the tea, setting out the blanket under the oak, and
organizing the Scriptures.

I joined them in the field for a picnic: fresh vegetables from my
garden, berries, warm bread, and sweet tea.

It was a holy, quiet afternoon. Just the four of us, sharing
stories of what God was doing, singing soft worship songs,
signing lyrics with hands raised to the sky. Silent prayers
carried in the breeze.

Then — **a sudden sound**.

From the road beyond the trees — a loud crash, the screech of
tires, metal against metal.

We all froze for a second. Maggie's face turned pale.

We rose together, rushing through the field and down the gravel path to the road.

There, at the edge of the fence, was a small car crumpled into a tree. Smoke rose from the hood. The door was bent. Inside, a young woman — blood on her forehead, dazed, trapped.

Maggie didn't hesitate.
 **"Call 911,"** she said firmly.

Then she ran to the woman, speaking calm words, reaching through the broken window to hold her hand.

I came beside her and began praying out loud, declaring life, peace, and protection in Jesus' name.

Keisha and Alondra stood nearby; hands raised in silent intercession.

The woman was conscious but panicking. Maggie whispered, **"You're not alone. We're here. Jesus is with you."**

When the ambulance arrived, the paramedics took over. But as they loaded her into the vehicle, the woman looked at Maggie and said weakly, **"You prayed... I felt peace."**

And just like that, Spirit showed me all again:

**Discipleship isn't just about studying.**
 **It's about being _ready_ — in season and out.**
 **To show up. To pray. To carry peace into chaos.**

That night, after everything had settled, the girls and I sat quietly on the porch again.

Maggie looked at me with wide eyes.
 **"I didn't know we'd be needed like that... I didn't even think — I just moved."**

I signed, smiling,
**"That's what a disciple does. You're listening now. Following His Spirit. That's growth. That's grace."**

And once again, I thanked my Heavenly Father.

**For protection.**
 **For His perfect timing.**
 **For daughters who walk in love and truth.**

## 12. Full Circle Grace

Two weeks have passed since the accident. The farm had returned to its rhythm — chickens clucking at dawn, dogs wagging their tails, herbs drying on hooks near the kitchen.

Then, one quiet afternoon, I heard the crunch of tires on gravel.

A small gray car pulled up. Slowly, the driver stepped out —
bandage still on her forehead, moving a little carefully, but with
purpose.

It was **the woman from the accident**.

I stepped out to greet her. Maggie followed behind, eyes wide in
recognition.

**"Hi..."** the woman said softly.
**"I don't know why, but I couldn't stop thinking about
this place. About you all. The way you prayed. I felt...
something I've never felt. Peace. Love. Not fear."** I
smiled and welcomed her in.

Her name was **Janelle**. She was in her early 30s. No church
background. She grew up with hurt, confusion, and silence from
heaven.

But that day on the road, something had broken through.

**"I didn't come here for anything big,"** she said, sipping
herbal tea at the kitchen table.
**"I just... need to know what it was I felt. And why you
were so calm."**

I nodded slowly and invited Maggie to speak.

Maggie told her story.

How she came to this farm was broken. How she learned about the love of Jesus — not religion, but relationship. How peace doesn't mean life is easy, but that I know who walks with you. She told her about surrender. About forgiveness. About freedom.

Janelle listened with tears quietly falling down her cheeks.

I invited her outside — under the same oak tree where so many moments had already unfolded. Maggie laid out a blanket. I brought out my Bible.

And then the Spirit began to move.

Janelle started to weep deeply. Not just from emotion, but from a soul finally **opening** to the truth.
 **"I didn't know I was carrying so much pain,"** she said through sobs.

**"I don't want to live in fear anymore."**

I laid hands on her shoulders.
 Maggie knelt beside her.
 Keisha and Alondra had already arrived earlier that day — I called them over.

Together, we all prayed.
 **You broke off lies, trauma, fear, and rejection in Jesus' name.**
 I watched as the Lord did what only He can do — poured His Spirit into the wounded places of her heart.

And when Janelle lifted her head, her face had changed.

Not just relief. **Radiance.**

She laughed through her tears.
**"I feel... clean. Light. Alive."**

I smiled and signed slowly,
**"That's what it feels like to be born again."**


Later, as the sun dipped low, we all sang on the porch — soft songs of worship. Janelle joined, unsure of the lyrics, but smiling wide.

And I remembered once more:

The farm was never just mine.
It was a field planted by the Lord.
A place where seeds of faith grow, where hearts are mended, and where strangers become daughters.

## 13. A Day of New Birth

One morning, as the sky glowed with golden light and the dew still clung to the grass, Maggie and I sat together on the porch.

I had been praying, asking the Lord about next steps — and in my spirit, it was clear.

It was time.

I turned to Maggie and signed with a smile:

**"Would you like to be baptized?**
**To go all in — water and Spirit?**
**To seal what God has done in you?"**

Maggie's eyes grew wide, and her hands trembled slightly with joy.

**"Yes!"** she signed quickly.

**"I've been waiting... I just didn't know if I was ready. But I feel it now — I want to bury the old me forever and be filled with His Spirit."**

We both wept together, giving thanks.  Later

that afternoon, Janelle returned.

 She was quiet, thoughtful, carrying a notebook full of Scriptures she had been reading on her own.

Over tea, Maggie told her the news — about the baptism.

Janelle's eyes filled with tears.

**"I want that too,"** she whispered.

**"I want this heaviness off me. I want to belong fully to Jesus. No turning back."**

I knew this wasn't just any ordinary day. This was holy ground.

I made some calls.

My best friend — a sister in Christ who had prayed with me for years — was thrilled. She agreed to come to the farm, along with a few others: trusted friends, women who understood the weight of deliverance and the joy of new life. We all would gather for worship, teaching, and prayer before the baptism.

## 14. Gospel Before the water Baptism

That Saturday came quickly.

The sun was warm, the animals peaceful, the farm felt alive with anticipation. A soft breeze moved through the trees as women arrived, bringing food, hugs, Bibles, and joyful hearts.

I gathered beneath the big oak tree once again. Everyone sat on picnic blankets or chairs in a circle, and I began to share:

What baptism truly means.
That it's not just a symbol — it's **death to sin, and new life in Christ**.

That it's a covenant, a surrender, and an invitation to walk in step with the Holy Spirit.

I read from Romans 6:
**"We were therefore buried with Him through baptism into death... in order that... we too may live a new life."**

Then my best friend stood and shared her testimony.
Another sister spoke of deliverance.
Together, the group prayed — worship songs rising, the Spirit thick and sweet.

Maggie sat with her eyes closed, smiling, ready.

Janelle wept softly, shaking as peace fell on her like rain.

And when it was time, I led them both down the small path that curved behind the garden — to the quiet stream that ran through my land.

## 15. Into the Water

The water was clear, cool, and holy.

Everyone stood on the bank, singing softly.
I stepped into the stream, barefoot on smooth stones, and invited Maggie first.

She waded in, hands trembling, eyes lifted to heaven.

**"Do you believe that Jesus Christ is Lord?"** I asked.
She nodded, heart full.
 **"Do you choose to die with Him — and rise
in His resurrection?"** **"Yes,"** she signed.

With my sister in Christ beside me, I lowered her into the water.

**"Maggie, I baptize you in the name of Jesus to death
and to rise with a new body in the name Jesus Amen."**

She came up laughing, crying — filled with joy. And as hands
reached out to her, I and the others laid hands on her and
prayed:

**"Holy Spirit, come."**

And He did.

Maggie fell to her knees on the shore, speaking in soft, beautiful
signs, a light on her face that could only come from heaven.

Then Janelle stepped forward. She was nervous, but steady.

The same questions. The same water.

When she rose, she gasped — and began to weep, then *shout*:
**"I'm free. I'm free!"**


Everyone clapped and sang. The Spirit moved.

I stood watching, overwhelmed. Not with pride — but with awe. That farm, this quiet piece of land, was being used as a holy place of transformation.

**Two daughters reborn.**
**Two flames ignited.**
**One Kingdom, forever growing.**

That night, around the fire pit, we all worshiped in unity — hands lifted, songs rising into the night sky.

And in my heart, once again, I whispered:

**"Thank You, Heavenly Father.**
**This is all Yours.**
**And it's only the beginning."**

# 16. Growing Through the Pain

The days after the baptisms were full of joy **and**

**wonder**.

I watched as Maggie and Janelle sat together on the porch, Bible opens between them, sometimes signing, sometimes praying, often laughing.

They were hungry — not just for knowledge, but for the **presence of the Lord**.

I gave Maggie a gentle nudge one morning.

**"You've grown strong, daughter. You're ready to pour into someone else."**

She looked surprised, then smiled wide. **"Me? Teach Janelle?"**

I nodded, signing slowly. **"She looks at you now. And you walk beside her, not above her. Just like Jesus walks with us."**

She took it to heart. Maggie began spending more time in the Word, preparing little notes and Scriptures to share. Her heart bloomed as she saw Janelle's faith deepen too.

But not long after, **the testing came.**

One warm, golden afternoon, Keisha and Alondra came back to visit the farm. They hadn't been around much lately, especially Keisha. She'd grown distant ever since Maggie began spending more time with me—mentoring, praying, walking in a bold new faith.

At first, everything seemed light. Laughs. Small talk. But something was off. Janelle could feel it—tension beneath the surface.

Maggie was glowing as she shared what the Lord was doing. How she felt led by the Spirit. How alive she felt now.

Then came the sharp words.

**"You think you're better than me now?"**
Keisha's voice was low but laced with bitterness.
**"All this Holy Spirit stuff... sounds like you drank too much of that church Kool-Aid."**

Maggie's smile faltered. Her eyes flicked to Janelle, uncertain.

**"Keisha..."** she began, but Keisha was already grabbing her bag.

**"I just came to see how you were doing. Guess I got my answer. I'm not into all this. It's too much. Too weird."**

She turned to go—and Alondra, silent the whole time, hesitated... then followed her without a word.

No hugs. No goodbye.

Just the sound of their footsteps fading down the gravel drive.

Maggie sank onto the porch steps, stunned. Silent tears trailing down her cheeks.

I came and sat beside her. No rush.
No fixing. Just presence. I gently
placed my hand over hers.

She signed, voice shaking,
**"I didn't mean to push them away. I just... I wanted to share the truth. Why did they get so angry?"**

50

I looked at her with a love that carried weight.
 **"Because child... the light you carry now exposes darkness in others. And some people aren't ready for that light."**

She nodded slowly, eyes wet.

I continued,
 **"You can't walk both roads—one with the world, and one with Christ. When you truly follow Jesus, you will**

**lose people. But the Lord sees your pain. And He will bring others who will stand with you."**

Then I smiled gently and said the words she needed:
 **"Remember what Jesus said in Luke 14— 'Whoever does not carry their cross and follow Me cannot be My disciple.'"**

Maggie wiped her face, took a deep breath, and whispered:  **"I still choose Him. Even if it hurts."**

That night, she and Janelle worshipped quietly. There were no crowds, no loud voices — just two young women choosing the narrow road

And I? I watched with a full heart.

Because I knew — this was
the mark of a true disciple:
Not how high they praise in
joy, but how steady they walk
through sorrow.

## 17. The Quiet and the Call

The morning air was crisp as Maggie and Janelle loaded their bags into the car. They were headed off to a week-long **disciple training camp** — a gathering of believers eager to go deeper, to be equipped for healing, deliverance, preaching, and walking fully in the Spirit.

I hugged them both before they left, my hands resting on their shoulders as I signed a blessing:

52

**"Go boldly. Let the Spirit teach you.**

**You're not going to learn more religion — you're going to learn to walk like Jesus."**

Maggie beamed. Janelle was nervous, but excited.

As their car disappeared down the road, the farm returned to a gentle rhythm.

Chicken clucked. Dogs followed every step. The garden was blooming. I spent long mornings in prayer, afternoons tending to the animals, and quiet evenings on the porch, worshiping with the sunset.

But then, one day, without warning, **Keisha showed up**.

I saw her car pull in — slow, uncertain.

She stepped out, not with her usual confidence, but with a hesitation that told me something inside her had shifted.

I stepped off the porch and approached her gently.

**"Hello, Keisha."**

She avoided my eyes at first, then looked around.

**"Is... is Maggie here?"**

I smiled kindly and signed, **"No, she's away at a discipleship training. Learning how to follow Jesus more deeply."**

Keisha looked surprised, maybe even disappointed.

**"She didn't tell me…"** she muttered.
Then she paused, standing still.
**"I thought maybe she would call. Or text. But nothing."**

I nodded slowly. There was more in her tone than she was letting on.

**"Would you like to leave a note?"** I asked gently.
**"A message for her?"**

Keisha hesitated… but then shook her head.

**"Nah. I was just checking. It's fine."**

She turned back toward the car.

But I saw the look in her eyes — something was stirring beneath the surface.

**Conflict.**
**Conviction.**
**A crack in the wall around her heart.**

As she drove away, I stayed at the edge of the porch, eyes on the gravel road.

Then, I went back inside and knelt by my bed.

And I prayed.

Not just soft words — but deep intercession.
For **Keisha's soul**.
For her heart to be softened.

For the wounds she carried, the pride that masked her pain, the truth that still hadn't broken through.

I spoke her name aloud to the Father. **"She's still Yours, Lord. Call her. Chase her. Don't let her go."**

The wind moved gently outside my window.

The dogs rested near my feet.

And in my spirit, I heard the whisper:

**"I'm not done with her yet."**

## 18. Joy Returns to the Farm

One week passed — and though the farm stayed peaceful, I missed them.

Maggie and Janelle.

Each day I prayed for them by name. That they would be stretched, taught, and set even more on fire for the Lord. I knew the kind of transformation that happens when hearts are fully surrendered and given room to grow.

And finally — they returned.

I noticed the car before I saw them. Laughter floated down the gravel road as they pulled in, waving excitedly.

I opened my arms wide, smiling from ear to ear as Maggie leapt from the car and hugged me tight. Janelle followed, glowing like sunlight, her spirit soft but bright.

**"We have so much to tell you!"** Maggie signed with excitement.

I welcomed them inside just as my **best friend and sister in Christ** arrived, carrying a big basket of food and her warm smile.

Soon the table was full — food, open Bibles, tearful laughter, deep stories.

Maggie shared how at camp she laid hands on a young woman and **watched her get healed** of pain she'd carried for years.

Janelle shared how she had struggled with fear, but during worship one night, she felt the presence of God so strong she fell to her knees — and **the fear left her**.

My friend clapped her hands,
tears in her eyes.
**"Look what the Lord has
done!"** she said.

That night, I didn't want to rush anything.

I sat around the table long after the food was gone, the oil lamp flickering gently. I talked about spiritual gifts, about listening to the Holy Spirit, about guarding the heart and walking humbly. I sang softly together, lifting worship into the stillness of the farm.

By the time the clock neared midnight, the stars were out, and the crickets had taken up their song.

Janelle stood, stretching.

**"I probably should drive home,"** she said, though she looked tired.

I put a gentle hand on her shoulder.

**"No need, daughter. Stay here tonight. There's peace in this place. Rest."**

She smiled and nodded, visibly relieved.

I led her to the guest room — now lovingly called "the disciples' room" — and made sure she was comfortable.

As I turned out the lights and walked back through the quiet house, my heart was full.

**Two young women who were once searching... now walking in the Spirit.**

**This home, once quiet and still... now filled**

**with joy, worship, and testimony.**

I stepped onto the porch, looked up at the stars, and whispered into the night:

**"Thank You, Father.**
**This is what I prayed for.   And You are**
**faithful."**

## 19. Janelle's Dream

The sun rose gently the next morning, casting soft gold through the guest room window. Birds sang, and the air carried the smell of fresh dew and warm earth.

Janelle stirred awake, but something in her spirit felt different.

She sat up slowly, her hands trembling. Her heart was still heavy — not with fear, but with a **holy weight**. She looked around the quiet room and whispered: "**Lord... what was that?**"

The dream had felt **so real**.

She came to find me in the kitchen, where I was already up, humming a praise song while preparing tea. I looked at her face and immediately knew.

**"You had a dream."**

She nodded and sat down at the table.
 **"I think it was from God. Can I share it with you?"**

I poured her a warm cup, sat across from her, and gave her my full attention.

**"In the dream," Janelle began, signing and speaking slowly,**
 **"I was standing in the middle of a wheat field. The wind was blowing, but I wasn't afraid. I saw Maggie and you standing far off, waving for me to come. But I couldn't move. I looked down — my feet were tangled in weeds."**

**"Then I heard a voice — so strong but gentle — say, 'You must forgive to be free."**

**"I looked up and suddenly, I was in a river.**

**The water was clear and flowing, and I was floating.**

 **It washed over my face, my hands, my heart... And I felt something *lift* off me."**

**"When I stood up from the water, the field was different. The weeds were gone. The path was open. I could walk toward the light."**

As she finished, tears filled her eyes.

I reached across the table and gently took her hand.

**"That was not just a dream, Janelle.
That was a vision.  The Lord
is calling you to forgive — to
release the pain, so you can
walk fully in freedom."**

She nodded slowly.

**"There's someone... in my past. I've tried to forget. But I think I've been carrying weight of it. Even through the joy, I feel it sometimes — like a shadow."**

I wasn't surprised. Often, as the Holy Spirit draws someone closer, He also brings things to the surface that need healing.  I offered to pray with her.

And as I laid hands on her and began to pray, the atmosphere shifted. The peace of God filled the room. Janelle wept quietly — a deep, healing cry. Not of fear, but of release.

She didn't say much afterward. But her face was different.
**Lightened. Softened. Free.**

Later, Maggie returned from a walk and found the two of me sitting together on the porch.

I didn't need to explain anything.
 The Spirit was already speaking to her too.

She hugged Janelle and said:
 **"You look like someone who's been washed by the river."**

And Janelle laughed through her tears.
 **"That's because I have."**

## 20. Fellowship at the Neighbor's House

A few days after Janelle's powerful dream and healing moment, my neighbors — a kind, older couple down the road — stopped by the farm.

Their eyes were full of warmth, their arms carrying a homemade cobbler and a folded invitation.

**"We're hosting a fellowship at our place this weekend,"** they said.
 **"Just a simple potluck, music, and testimonies. Would love for you and the girls to come."**

I smiled, grateful.

It felt like **God was weaving threads together**, calling His people closer.

I told Maggie and Janelle later that evening, and both lit up with excitement.

**"A chance to meet more people who walk with Jesus?"** Maggie signed. **"And food?"** Janelle added with a grin.

The day of the fellowship came, and the sun was shining brightly.

I brought my famous herb chicken, a big bowl of roasted vegetables from my garden, and a few jars of homemade tea.

As I pulled up to the neighbor's house, I was welcomed by the sound of laughter, acoustic guitar, and the delicious aroma of good food.

Long tables stretched under shade trees. Children played nearby. Plates were already being filled. Strangers smiled like old friends.

**This is what the Kingdom looks like,** I thought. **Not just buildings and pews, but hearts open around the table.**

After everyone had eaten and settled, someone strummed a guitar and began softly singing a worship song.

Soon, hands lifted, eyes closed. Some people wept. Some just smiled. But the **presence of God was unmistakable**.

Then the testimonies began.

One by one, people stood and shared pieces of their lives:

- A woman who had battled addiction for years and was now free.

- A man who had once been angry and bitter, now gentle and healed after forgiving his father.

- A teenager who had been silently suicidal, now full of hope after encountering Jesus in a dream.

Each story was different.
Each one **marked by the same hand** — the hand of the Savior.

Then something beautiful happened.

Janelle stood.

She didn't plan to. But her heart was moved.

Her voice was soft, but steady.

**"I had a dream. And it showed me I needed to forgive. I thought I had buried it, but it was still holding me down. And God... He set me free. I didn't even know how much I needed it — but now, I feel like I can breathe again."** There was a holy silence.

And then, quiet applause.

Nods. Tears. Smiles.

Maggie put her arm around her, beaming with pride.

Later, as the sun began to set and the gathering wound down, one woman approached me quietly.

**"I needed to hear her story. I've been holding onto something too. I think it's time to let go."**

I nodded gently.

Because I knew — this wasn't just a potluck. It was a **divine appointment**.

And the Lord had come to **heal more than just one heart**.

## 21. The One Who Stayed Behind

The sun had dipped below the trees, and most guests had begun to leave the neighbor's fellowship. Laughter still echoed across the lawn as people packed up dishes and hugged goodbye.

But one woman — quiet, middle-aged, her eyes burdened with something heavy — lingered near the fence.

I noticed her standing alone, her hands clenched, shoulders tight.

I walked slowly, Maggie and Janelle close behind. I greeted her with a warm smile, and she offered a weak one in return.

**"My name's Denise,"** she said.
Her voice was low, almost ashamed.
**"I... I almost didn't come today. But something told me I needed to."**

She paused, looking down at her hands.

**"When your friend Janelle spoke about forgiveness and freedom... something in me cracked. I've been living with so much torment. Nightmares. Anxiety. Anger that I can't control. I've tried counseling, medication, even church. But nothing helped."**

Her eyes filled with tears.

**"I think there's something deeper. I think I need... deliverance."**

The air went still.

I stepped forward gently and signed with care and authority:

**"Jesus can set you free.
If you're willing, we can pray with you right now."**

She nodded, trembling.
**"Please."**

I found a quiet corner near the trees. Maggie and Janelle came with me, and my neighbor — the host — joined too.

I sat Denise down, gently laid a hand on her shoulder, and began to pray in the Spirit. The atmosphere changed immediately — thick with **power and peace**.

Maggie softly worshipped beside me.
Janelle whispered Scripture over her.
My neighbor anointed her forehead with oil.

At first, Denise simply cried.

Then, as the prayer went deeper, she began to shake. Old pain began to surface — lies spoken over her, abuse from her past, the hatred she'd carried in silence.

As I prayed, I felt a push in my spirit.

**"Spirit of fear, go.
Spirit of torment, go.
 In Jesus' name, be free."**

Denise gasped.

Suddenly her body was stilled, and a **wave of peace** washed over her face.

Tears streamed down, but this time they were not from pain — they were from **release**.

She opened her eyes slowly and whispered,
 **"It's gone. I don't feel heavy anymore. I feel... clean."**

I nodded, smiling through my own tears.

"That's the love of Jesus.
 He doesn't just save, He delivers.
 He breaks chains."

Denise looked at all of us, stunned.
 "Can I come visit your farm sometime? I think I
need to learn more... about this Jesus I thought I
already knew." I squeezed her hand.

"You are always welcome."

---

That night, back on my porch under a sky full of stars, Maggie
whispered:

"I never thought I'd see that with my own eyes. That
wasn't just a story in the Bible. That was real."

I nodded, holding my tea close.

"It's always been real.
 Now you're walking in it.
 This is just the beginning."

## 22. Denise Prepares for Baptism

A few days had passed since that powerful evening at the neighbor's fellowship, and Denise had not stopped thinking about what she felt — the lightness in her chest, the peace that replaced the weight of years of sorrow. She had tasted freedom, and now she wanted more.

So, when I called to check in and gently asked,

**"Denise, do you feel ready for baptism?"**

**She didn't hesitate.**

**"Yes,"**

**she said, her voice clear.**
**"I don't want to wait anymore. I want to walk in this fully."**

---

The next morning, Denise came to the farm. The skies were wide and blue; the air was soft with warmth. Maggie and Janelle helped prepare a quiet space in the backyard — nothing fancy, just peaceful and sacred.

Before anything, I sat together on the porch with warm tea in hand. The birds sang in the background, and the Holy Spirit was already near.

I opened the Word, signing and speaking with calm and clarity:

**"Before we baptize you, Denise, we want to make sure you understand what this means. This isn't a ritual. This is a burial of the old self... and a resurrection into new life with Jesus."**

Denise nodded, fully attentive.

**"Have you repented?" you asked gently.**

Her eyes welled up with emotion.

**"Yes. I've already started. But I know there's more I need to let go. Can we pray through it together?"**

So, the three of us sat close, and with love and patience, I led her in a quiet, powerful time of repentance.

She confessed things she had never said aloud — bitterness she'd carried, the shame she had buried, lies she believed about herself.

And with every word, she began to loosen her grip on the past.

I saw in her eyes — the release, the surrender.

When she finished, Janelle quietly handed her a small white cloth and whispered,
**"You're about to step into freedom."**

---

I walked together to the little pond near the edge of my property.

The water was still, surrounded by trees and open sky. I had baptized others here before — and each time, Heaven rejoiced.

Maggie stood ready to record for Denise if she wanted it later, and Janelle sang softly in the background, a simple chorus:

**"I have decided to follow Jesus..."**

I stepped into the water with Denise, holding her hands.

**"Denise, have you confessed Jesus Christ as your Lord and Savior?"**

**"Yes."**

**"Do you believe He died for your sins and rose again, giving you new life?"**

**"Yes, I do."**

**"Then by your confession of faith, I baptize you in the name of Jesus to death and rise with a new body in name Jesus Amen."**

I lowered her gently into the water.

And when she rose — her face shone.

Tears streamed down her cheeks, but they were not from sorrow.

They were holy tears of rebirth.

Maggie and Janelle clapped and praised God. I hugged her as she stepped onto the shore, wrapped in a soft towel, reborn.

Denise looked out over the trees and sky, whispering,

**"I feel brand new."**

I nodded with joyful heart. **"Because**

**you are."**

## 23. Washed in His Love

 The evening was warm and quiet, the kind of stillness that feels like a blanket from Heaven. A few days had passed since Denise's baptism, and tonight, I invited her—and a few others—back to the farm for something simple: worship and rest.

No formal service. No set plan.

Just voices, hearts, and Jesus.

We gathered in the living room, where lanterns cast soft light on the wooden beams. Maggie strummed her guitar gently. Janelle sat beside Denise, both barefoot and peaceful. I poured tea and settled in with the others, creating a circle of comfort.

Maggie began singing a hymn—slow, familiar, and full of truth:

**"I am washed, I am washed, I am drenched in love..."**

Denise closed her eyes, her hands resting in her lap.

But when Janelle joined in, her voice steady and anointed, something broke open in Denise's chest.

Tears rolled down her cheeks, not from pain—but from a deep release.

I reached for her hand.

I signed gently:
 **"You're free to worship now, Denise. Not to earn love— but because you already have it."**

She looked at me, trembling.

"I never thought I could be this open. I've always watched other people lift their hands... but I never believed I was welcome."

I signed again, slowly and with care: **"You are.**

**You always were."**

And slowly, she stood.

Not rushed, not pressured.

Just willing.

She lifted her hands, eyes shut, heart open. And the whole room shifted.

The Spirit of God filled the space—not loud, but weighty.

Maggie played quieter now. Janelle stopped singing to pray under her breath.

I signed over Denise: **"You are not broken. You are beloved. You are free."**

Someone whispered, **"Amen."**

And at that moment, Denise began to sway. Not to the music, but to the rhythm of healing.

When the song ended, she sat down again, smiling through the tears.

**"I didn't know worship could be this real,"** she said. **"It's like... love keeps washing over me. Even after the water."**

I nodded; my own eyes misted.

**"Because it does."**

## 24. The Unseen Wound

A few weeks had passed since Denise's baptism. She had begun attending local prayer meetings, reading her Bible each morning, and spending weekends at the farm learning how to walk as a disciple.

Everything seemed steady—until the phone call.

Denise received news that her estranged mother, whom she had not spoken to in over ten years, was terribly ill and in hospital.

When she arrived at the farm the next day, she looked like she hadn't slept.

I welcomed her into the kitchen, and after a quiet breakfast, she finally said:

**"She wants to see me. My mother. The woman who never wanted me, who blamed me for everything... she says she's sorry now."**

Her voice trembled with pain and confusion.

**"I don't know if I can do it. I thought I forgave her. But now that I might have to look her in the eyes, something in me resists. I feel like a child again. Small. Wounded."**

I sat beside her in silence for a while, letting the Holy Spirit fill the space.

Then I signed gently:

**"Forgiveness doesn't always mean trust or closeness again. But sometimes, God asks us to go back—not to reopen the wound, but to show how He's healed it."**
Denise looked at me with tears forming.

**"I'm scared I'll fall apart. What if I get angry again? What if I can't show grace?"**

**"Then take Jesus with you,"** I said gently. **"You're not the same woman who left that house. And you don't walk in there alone anymore."**

I offered to pray over her, and Janelle joined, laying hands on her shoulders while Maggie quietly sang a hymn in the next room.

The presence of God came soft and strong.

I declared strength and clarity over Denise, speaking truth into the shaky places of her heart.

Before she left that day, she turned and said:

**"Even if it's hard, I'll go. Not because I want to, but because He forgave me first. I want to be free, totally free."**

I nodded, heart full of both burden and hope.

**"Freedom always costs something. But it's worth it."**

## 25. A Healing Visit

Two days after Denise left for the hospital, my phone buzzed. It was a simple text:

**"Can I come over tomorrow? I need to talk."**

I replied, *"Of course. The porch is waiting."*

The next afternoon, Denise arrived quietly. Her face looked tired, but her spirit... steadier.

I handed her a cup of warm tea and sat beside her as the wind stirred the tall grass.

She spoke slowly. **"I**

**went. I saw her."**

She paused.

**"It wasn't like I imagined. She looked so small... so weak. She didn't even remember everything she had done. But when I walked in, I didn't feel the old anger. I felt sorrow. And I felt something else."**

She glanced at me with awe in her eyes.

**"I felt compassion. Not mine. His."**

Tears filled my eyes as she continued.

**"I told her I forgave her. She cried. I prayed for her. It was simple. Not dramatic. But something broke in me. Something that had lived there for years. And when I left... I felt peace."**

I reached over and squeezed her hand.

**"That is freedom, Denise. You didn't just forgive — you released the pain to God. That's what healing looks like."**

She smiled, eyes soft but strong.

**"I used to think being a believer meant showing up to church and trying not to sin too much. Now I know... it means dying to yourself, over and over, and trusting that Jesus will carry you through the hard things."**

Just then, Maggie and Janelle returned from a walk with the dogs. As they came up the steps, Denise looked at them and said:

**"I'm ready to help. I want to serve others, too. I want to be there for someone the way you all were for me."**

I nodded, feeling the Spirit stir again.

**"Then get ready. There's always someone. And the Lord will use every tear, every healing, for His glory."**

As the four of us sat together on the porch that evening — sipping tea, laughing gently, and sharing hearts — you knew: this was the church.

Not just a building, but a family. A gathering of the healed and healing. A place where grace lived and grew.

And this was just the beginning.

# 26. The Long Road Ahead

A few days after Denise's baptism, the rhythm of the farm returned — peaceful mornings with chickens, the dogs chasing butterflies, the soft scrape of garden tools in the earth, and long evenings on the porch with tea and prayers.

Maggie and Janelle had begun helping more each day, both in the garden and in the ministry. I could see their roots going deeper, not just in soil but in faith. Still, life has a way of testing what's been planted.

One morning, as dew still clung to the grass, Denise arrived early, her face pale and tense. I met her at the porch with open arms.

"Something wrong?" I signed gently.

She nodded and sat slowly on the top step. **"My sister found out I got baptized,"** she said.
**"She's furious. Says I've been brainwashed. Say I'm walking away from our family."**

I listened quietly. Her words weren't just about hurting, they were about choice, the cost of obedience.

**"I never thought following Jesus would make me feel so... alone,"** she whispered.

I nodded slowly, then reached for her hand.

**"You're not alone,"** I signed. **"Jesus said the road would be narrow. But He also promised to walk it with us."**

Denise wiped her eyes. **"I don't want to go back to who I was. I don't. But it hurts when people I love don't understand."**

I looked out at the morning sun rising over the field. **"Let your roots grow deep. This farm isn't just a place of rest. It's a training ground. The world may shake, but if you're rooted in Him, you won't fall."**

Just then, Maggie came outside with a basket of warm bread. Janelle followed, holding a thermos of tea. No words needed — just presence.

They sat down beside Denise, offering quiet companionship. The kind Jesus gives through His people.

And as I passed the bread around, I was reminded again:

Discipleship isn't just revival and miracles — it's walking with people through the fire, loving them when it costs, and helping them stand again when the world tries to pull them down.

The narrow road may be long — but none of us would ever walk it alone.

## 27. The Visitor in the Rain

The rain had come suddenly that afternoon, washing the dust from the trees and turning the fields into soft, shimmering gold. I was inside preparing stew for dinner when the dogs barked — not alarmed, just alert.

I stepped onto the porch and saw a figure at the gate — drenched in the rain, hood pulled low. I called out gently, motioning for them to come in from the weather.

As the person stepped closer, I realized it was **Keisha**.

Her eyes were swollen from crying. She looked lost, tired, and completely unguarded for the first time.

**"I didn't know where else to go,"** she said, voice shaking. **"I thought I was fine. I thought I didn't need any of this. But I've been having nightmares. My job's a mess. I'm so angry all the time. And Maggie..."** Her voice broke. **"I said awful things to her."**

I didn't say much. I just stepped aside and opened the door.

**"Come in,"** I signed. **"You're welcome here."**

Inside, the house was warm with the smell of herbs and soup. Janelle came from the other room, surprised but quick to show grace. Maggie stepped in next, her face unsure — old pain flickering — but she didn't turn away.

Keisha lowered her head.

**"I'm sorry."**

Maggie's voice was soft. **"I forgive you."**

It wasn't emotional — it was deep. A choice of love over pride. Grace over hurt.

I could feel the Spirit of God settle over the house like a blanket.

That night, we all sat together — no preaching, no pressure. Just food, quiet music, and presence.

Later, Keisha sat by the fire. She looked at me with exhausted eyes.

**"Can people like me really change? I've always been the strong one. The loud one. The angry one. I don't even know who I am anymore."**

I knelt by her side and signed slowly:

**"You are loved. And the strongest thing you'll ever do... is surrender."**

A single tear slid down her cheek.

**"Then I want to try."**

The rain outside slowed to a drizzle, but in that quiet house, something had shifted — a heart had turned.

I smiled to myself, grateful once again for the porch, the people, and the promise.

This farm wasn't just a place of peace.

It was a place of **rebirth**.

## 28. Seeds in the Firelight

The next morning brought a deep stillness. The kind that doesn't just settle over the land, but into the soul.

Keisha stayed in the guest room, and I let her sleep late — healing sometimes starts with rest. Meanwhile, the house came alive gently: tea brewing, dogs stretching, the chickens clucking their morning chorus.

Maggie and Janelle helped prepare a small breakfast — sweet cornbread, fresh fruit, and herb tea from the garden. When Keisha finally came to the table, her eyes were clearer, her body lighter. She was quieter than usual, almost like she was listening to something new in her heart.

Later that afternoon, I all sat beneath the willow tree near the garden, the sun slipping through its long branches like gold ribbon.

I pulled out the small wooden box I kept near the porch. Inside there were a few things I often used in teaching: a mustard seed, a small oil vial, slips of Scripture, and tiny slips of paper for personal prayer.

I handed Keisha a seed.

She turned it over in her hand, brow furrowed. **"It's so small."**

I nodded. **"So is faith, in the beginning. But give it the right soil — honesty, surrender, and the love of God — and it becomes something no storm can uproot."**

Then I asked each of them to write something, they were asking the Lord to grow in them.

Janelle wrote: **"Courage to speak the truth."**
Maggie: **"Wisdom to lead others."**
Keisha hesitated, then wrote with trembling fingers: **"A new heart."**

I prayed over them one by one. Not long, not loud — just steady. Like rain soaking into dry ground.

As dusk fell and the stars began to blink into view, Keisha turned to me.

**"I want to learn more. I do not just want to visit. I want to understand what it means to really follow Him."**

I smiled, feeling that now-familiar tug of the Spirit: the drawing of another soul to the table.

**"You're already on the path,"** I said. **"And we'll walk it with you."**

That night, by the fire, Keisha laughed for the first time. Not forced — real. Maggie joined her, and Janelle sang softly, her voice rising like smoke into the dark sky.

And I sat back, tea in hand, grateful. These were not just guests anymore.

They were **disciples in bloom**.

And the farm, this quiet piece of land, had become a **field of revival**.

## 29. The Waters and the Word

The next few days were full of preparation — not just of meals or garden work, but of hearts. Keisha asked questions, deep ones, the kind that show the soil is finally soft enough to plant truth in.

She sat with Janelle each morning, reading Scripture. Walked with Maggie in the garden, asking about prayer. And at night, she sat on the porch with me, sharing pieces of her story that had long been buried.

**"I used to think faith was for weak people,"** she said one evening. **"But now I see... it takes more strength to trust than to fight."**

94

I nodded slowly, signing: **"Surrender isn't weakness. It is the door to real power."**

On the third day, Keisha stood in the center of the field behind the house, her hands lifted, her eyes full of tears.

**"I want to be baptized,"** she said.

Everyone gathered the next afternoon — Denise, Maggie, Janelle, my friend, and other sisters in Christ. The sky was a perfect blue, and the pond at the edge of the property shimmered in the sunlight.

I stepped into the water with Keisha, and she trembled — not from fear, but from reverence.

I asked gently, **"Keisha, do you believe Jesus is Lord?"**

She nodded, firmly. **"With all my heart."**

**"And do you renounce the world, the lies of the enemy, and surrender your life fully to Him?"**

Tears streamed down. **"Yes. I want to be free."**

And with the whole farm watching, with the Spirit of God thick in the air, I lowered her into the water — and raised her into new life.

The cheers and praise rang across the field. Maggie clapped with joy, Janelle danced barefoot in the grass, and Denise knelt in worship.

Keisha stepped out of the water glowing. Not just from the sun, but from **resurrection**.

## 30. The Porch and the Promise

That evening, everyone gathered on the porch again — the place where so many stories had begun.

Plates were passed; songs were sung. Testimonies flowed like sweet tea, and laughter rang like bells across the trees.

Keisha sat next to Denise, both of them shining. Maggie gently read from the Gospel of John, her voice steady and kind. Janelle played worship softly on her guitar, her voice now bolder, freer.

I looked around at this family the Lord had built.

Not perfect people. But **healed. Growing. Awake**.

And I felt the quiet voice of the Lord whisper again:

**"This is what I meant by 'follow Me.'
Not just services — but life.
Not just belief — but transformation.
Not just words — but fruit."**

I closed my eyes and breathed in the warm air.

This farm, this porch, these daughters — all part of a story much greater than my own.

I had been faithful with my field.
And He had been faithful with His promise.

Because when I live a life of surrender, even the quiet places become **holy ground**.

And the porch?

It was not just a resting place.

It was the beginning of a thousand new stories

## The Porch Is Still Open

You've come to the last page, but I pray the journey continues in your heart.

Though Maggie, Janelle, Denise, and the others are characters on a page, the healing they encountered, the voice they heard, and the baptism waters they stepped into are real for anyone who says yes to Jesus.

Maybe you saw yourself in the quiet strength.
Or the questions.
Or the breaking point.
Maybe you felt the porch breeze stir something deeper.

If you did—don't rush past it.

Jesus still meets people on porches and in wheat fields, in hospital rooms and kitchens, in dreams and in silence. He still calls the weary and the curious, the searching and the stuck.

He's calling you, too.


### A Closing Prayer

Jesus,
Thank You for the one holding this book.
You know their story, every chapter.
Let these fictional lives point them to the real, living hope that is You.
Heal what's broken. Awaken what's sleeping.
Draw them into deeper trust, deeper healing, deeper joy.
And remind them:
They are never
alone on the
porch. In name
Jesus, Amen.

—

*With love and hope,*
**Ashley Gill**
*Author – deaf woman, disciple, storyteller*

# Scripture Guide
*Verses to Remember from Each Chapter of*
**The Porch and the Promise**

1. **The Porch and the Stranger**

   Hebrews 13:2

   "Do not forget to show hospitality to strangers..."

2. **A Place to Begin Again**  Isaiah 43:19 "See, I am doing a new thing..."

3. **The Weeds and the Wheat**

   Matthew 13:30

   "Let both grow together until the harvest..."

4. **A Song in the Soil**

   Psalm 126:5

   "Those who sow with tears will reap with songs of joy."

5. **Janelle's Story**

   2 Corinthians 5:17

   "If anyone is in Christ, the new creation has come..."

6. **The Dream in the Field**

   Genesis 28:16

   "Surely the Lord is in this place..."

7. **A Disciple in Bloom**

   John 15:8

   "This is to my Father's glory, that you bear much fruit..."

8. **Maggie's Calling**
Matthew 28:19
"Go and make disciples of all nations…"

9. **The Invitation: From the Farm to the Nations** Acts
1:8
"You will be my witnesses… to the ends of the earth."

10. **Baptized in the River**
Romans 6:4 "…just as Christ was
raised… we too may live a new life."

11. **A Place for Denise**
Isaiah 61:1
"…to bind up the brokenhearted, to proclaim freedom…"

12. **The One Who Stayed Behind**
Luke 15:20
"…his father saw him and was filled with compassion…"

13. **Letters from Home**
2 Corinthians 5:20
"We are therefore Christ's ambassadors…"

14. **Through the Fire, together**
Isaiah 43:2
"When you walk through the fire, you will not be burned…"

15. **A Harvest in Winter**
Galatians 6:9
"At the proper time we will reap a harvest…"

### 16. Janelle's Dream

Joel 2:28
"Your old men will dream dreams…"

### 17. Carried by Grace

Deuteronomy 1:31
"…the Lord your God carried you…"

### 18. Planted by Streams

Psalm 1:3
"…a tree planted by streams of water…"

### 19. The Quiet Room

Psalm 91:1
"…dwells in the shelter of the Most High…"

### 20. When the Women Gather

Acts 16:13
"…we began to speak to the women who had gathered there."

### 21. The Table Set for All

Luke 14:23
"…compel them to come in, so that my house will be full."

### 22. Denise's Firelight Song   Psalm 40:3 "He put a new song in my mouth…"

### 23. Storm Season

Mark 4:39
"'Quiet! Be still!' Then the wind died down…"

### 24. Rooted and Rising

Colossians 2:7
"Rooted and built up in him…"

### 25. Mercy for the Reckless
Titus 3:5
"He saved us... because of his mercy..."

### 26. The Garden After Rain   Hosea 6:3 "He will come to us like the rain..."

### 27. When Forgiveness Blooms
Ephesians 4:32
"Be kind... forgiving each other..."

### 28. The Work of the Spirit
Zechariah 4:6
"'Not by might nor by power, but by my Spirit...'"

### 29. Sent Two by Two   Luke 10:1 "He sent them two by two..."

### 30. The Porch and the Promise
Hebrews 10:23
"...he who promised is faithful."

# Devotional 1 – Hearing God's Voice Key Bible Verse

*"And it shall come to pass in the last days, says God... your young men shall see visions, your old men shall dream dreams." — Acts 2:17 (NKJV)*

## Reflection Prompt

Has God ever spoken to your heart in a quiet way—through a dream, a person, or a stirring you couldn't explain? Are you open to hearing Him now?

## Prayer

Father, thank You for still speaking to us in personal and powerful ways. Help me to pay attention when You whisper to my spirit. Give me courage to follow You, even when the path is new or uncertain. Let my life be a testimony of Your grace and calling. Amen.

# Devotional 2 – Stepping Out in Faith

## Key Bible Verse

*"Trust in the Lord with all your heart and lean not on your own understanding; in all your ways acknowledge Him, and He shall direct your paths." — Proverbs 3:5–6 (NKJV)*

## Reflection Prompt

What step of faith is God asking you to take? What might be holding you back?

## Prayer

Lord, I don't have to understand everything to follow You. Give me faith that walks even when I cannot see the full road. Lead me step by step into Your promise. Amen.

## Devotional 3 – New Creation Key Bible Verse

*"Therefore, if anyone is in Christ, he is a new creation; old things have passed away; behold, all things have become new."*
*— 2 Corinthians 5:17 (NKJV)*

## Reflection Prompt

What part of your old life do you need to leave behind in the waters of grace? Can you receive the truth that you are new?

## Prayer

Jesus, thank You for washing me clean. I let go of the labels and burdens I once carried. Remind me daily that I am made new in You—beloved, free, and full of purpose. Amen.

## Devotional 4 – Living in Freedom Key Bible Verse

*"It is for freedom that Christ has set us free. Stand firm, then, and do not let yourselves be burdened again by a yoke of slavery." — Galatians 5:1 (NIV)*

## Reflection Prompt

Are there old voices or patterns trying to pull you back into bondage? How can you choose freedom today?

## Prayer

Lord, thank You for breaking every chain that bound me. When fear, shame, or rejection try to rise up, remind me that I belong to You now. I will walk forward in the freedom You died to give me. Amen.

## My Testimony

*1 Thessalonians 5:16–18 (ESV)*
*Rejoice always, pray without ceasing, give thanks in all circumstances; for this is the will of God in Christ Jesus for you.*

I did not always know how to rejoice. There were days when the pain was too thick, when prayers felt like whispers into the wind. But even then—God was near.
Even in silence, He was speaking. I look back now and see His hand steadying me when I should have fallen, carrying me through storms I did not think I would survive. I've learned that rejoicing isn't always loud, sometimes it's a quiet yes, a tearful thank you, a whispered prayer in the dark. This is my story, of how Jesus met me, healed me, and taught me to pray without ceasing, to give thanks even when it hurts, and to rejoice, always.

## When the Righteous Cry

*Psalm 34:17 (ESV)*
*When the righteous cry for help, the Lord hears and delivers them out of all their troubles.*

I cried for help not once, not twice but repeatedly, from places too deep for words. And He heard me. Not because I was strong, not because I was good, but because He is faithful. There were troubles that tried to bury me, memories that haunted, fears that pressed heavy on my chest. But the Lord didn't turn away. He came close. He delivered me piece by piece, teaching me that healing comes like morning light soft, slow, but certain.

I am here today not because the road was easy, but because Jesus never let go. I thank You,
Lord because He has been faithful to me through every step of this journey. This year, Jesus grew in me on the inside. Jesus deepened my spirit and gave me the gift of discernment. Jesus taught me how to wait with patience, how to walk in peace, how to rejoice in true joy, and how to hold on to hope.

I stepped forward in obedience to my Heavenly Father, walking in the ministry You placed before me. I turned away from the old life, repented, and chose to live renewed heart changed, eyes fixed on Jesus. Lord, this is what matters most to me: to walk with Him, to know Him, to love Him with my life.

And I continue to say Thank You, Amen.

To the stories that first lived in my heart, and to the quiet porch moments where they came to life.
May imagination always flows like water, and hope rise like clouds.

Beneath the hush of evening light, I opened stories, soft and bright.
And from their pages, skies took flight, with fields and faith and wings of might.

"Write the vision; make it plain on tablets, so he may run who reads it."
— Habakkuk 2:2 (ESV)

— Ashley Gill

**Artwork Thanks**
*Thank you to the artists and AI tools that contributed to the beautiful illustrations featured in this book. Your creativity and technology combined with these images into life in a unique way.*

Made in the USA
Columbia, SC
12 July 2025

60409994R00065